"The Ladybird
Has Broken Her Leg"

Magda M. Olchawska
Illustrated by Agata Boba

Other Books by Magda Olchawska

Mikolay & Julia Meet the Fairies
Mikolay & Julia In the Attic
Bear Gets a Beating
Moncania

First published in 2017

ISBN 978-83-946520-3-6

Visit Magda's websites:
www.magdaolchawska.com
www.atthetable.eu

This Book Belongs To

....

William is a little boy
who shares his bedroom
with a little spider.
His parents don't mind,
as long as William
looks after the spider,
and it stays in his room.

One day,
while chasing a snail
in the Botanic Garden,
William noticed a little Ladybird
sitting on a gigantic
green leaf, crying.

He went closer to the Ladybird.
"Why are you crying?" he asked.
"I think I broke my leg",
sobbed the little Ladybird.
"Can I see?" asked the boy.
"No, no..., I'm too scared of little boys.
You are going to pull my leg
like the other boy did",
she replied in a whisper
and started crying even harder.

"I promise I won't.
I love all the crawlies!!!
I even have a spider
living with me",
said William, giving the Ladybird
the nicest of his smiles
and showing her the picture
he took of his best friend,
the Spider.

"Is that your Spider?"
William nodded. The Ladybird
thought for a moment,
then looked closely at the boy,
who looked quite pleasant.
She showed him her leg. William looked
and looked and finally said,
"I need to take you to the doctor.
It looks like your leg is broken."
"I don't think the doctor
would like to see me. I'm only a bug",
replied the Ladybird, sadly.

"Oh, yes."
William became a bit gloomy.
"I know! I'm going to take you home
and look after you until you get better."
suggested the boy.
"Would you do that?" asked the Ladybird,
who had never met anyone
so kind before.
"Of course", he said. "Come on."
He lowered his finger
and with a bit of help
the Ladybird climbed up.

At home the little boy
opened one of his
"How to Care for the Crawlies"
books, which his parents
made for him
from all the information
they could gather.

In fact,
he had a book about almost
every crawly thing there was.
All of them were handmade
by his parents.
After studying the book
for a few minutes,
William started applying all sorts
of homemade medications
to speed up the healing process
for the Ladybird.

It took the whole night
to mend the tiny broken leg
of the Ladybird.
The next morning
she was as good as new.

In the end
the Ladybird
felt so comfortable
with William and the spider
she decided to stay
with the two of them
for good.

"The Ladybird Has Broken Her Leg"

by Magda Olchawska

Illustrated by Agata Boba

behance.net/agataboba

Check out Magda's websites:

www.magdaolchawska.com

www.atthetable.eu

To get in touch:
magda@magdaolchawska.com

info@atthetable.eu

To stay in touch:

instagram.com/m.olchawska/

twitter.com/magdaolchawska

facebook.com/magdaolchawska